This igloo book belongs to:

Eden

igloobooks

Published in 2021
First published in the UK by Igloo Books Ltd
An imprint of Igloo Books Ltd
Cottage Farm, NN6 0BJ, UK
Owned by Bonnier Books
Sveavägen 56, Stockholm, Sweden
www.igloobooks.com

0921 002
2 4 6 8 10 9 7 5 3
ISBN 978-1-80022-447-6

Written by Stephanie Moss
Illustrated by Francesca De Luca

Designed by Alice Dainty
Edited by Stephanie Moss

Printed and manufactured in China

CAKE
FOR
Breakfast

igloobooks

Today is my birthday.
It's finally here!
I wish it would come
more than one day a year.

There'll be lots of presents
and fun things to do.
I'll play with the streamers
and bright balloons, too.

We're having a party
with all of my friends.
And I love to open
the cards people send.

But my favourite bit
that I can't wait to see
is my birthday cake that
Mum's made just for me!

I jump out of bed...

... but there's no one awake.

So, I tiptoe downstairs to peek at my cake.

It's covered in sprinkles,
with candles on top.

Now I'm so excited,
I think I might pop!

Will anyone know if
I have one small bite?

Now I'm one year older
it might be alright!

So, I slowly

reach up
and then suddenly...

...SPLAT!

I've ruined my wonderful cake, just like that.

"**Oh, no!**"
I say softly.
"**What shall
I do now?**"

I need to
replace it.
But I don't
know how!

I look in the cupboards
and rummage around.
Then start mixing up all
the things that I've found.

Yummy! That ice cream
would taste nice in there.

UH-OH!

I think someone's
coming downstairs!

Mum gives me a kiss.

"Happy Birthday!" she cries. Then...

... SQUELCH!

She steps into a gooey surprise.

"... It looks like I'm making you two cakes this year!"

I start to feel bad and my cheeks turn bright red.
Then Mum puts a party hat onto my head.

"We'll bake it together," she says with a smile. "But no eating cake for breakfast for a while!"

CRACK-POUR-WHISK! GLUG-MIX! Can I lick the spoon? Then quick, in the oven... the party starts soon!

My friends **OOH** and **AAH** at my new birthday cake. But they don't know how much fun it was to make.

"Blow out the candles,"
my mum says to me.
I take a deep breath
as they count...

... one...

... two...

... THREE!

Everyone sings Happy Birthday together.
This has been my **VERY BEST** birthday ever!